My CTR Ring

Written by Michael Nelsen & Wendy Nelsen

Illustrated by Jodi Jensen

BOOKCRAFT

SALT LAKE CITY, UTAH

To Corinne, Jarin, Dallin, Alex, and AmiDayne Nelsen

for your love and inspiration

—MN & WN

Library of Congress Catalog Card Number 00-130109

ISBN 1-57345-467-2

Printed in the United States of America   18961-6435

10   9   8   7   6   5   4   3   2   1

This is my CTR ring
so shiny and so bright.
It helps me to remember
to always choose the right!

So read these little stories
about some special friends.
Take your time and you decide
just how each story ends.

Laurie had her favorite toy
when I came in to play.
"I want that toy," and she is small . . .
I'll take it right away.

But that would make my sister cry,
and Mom says, "Please don't fight!"

Should I choose the wrong
and take her toy—
Or share . . . and choose
the right?

Choose the right with all your might,
and things will go your way.
My CTR ring tells me so,
each and every day.

Where's your homework? Is it done?"
my teacher asked of me.
I hadn't done it, but I said,
"Well, ma'am, . . . let me see . . ."

So many little stories
circled in my head.
Monsters ate my homework,
or maybe my dog Fred.

I see her eyes; she's trusting me,
believing every word.

Do I choose the wrong and tell a lie—
Or choose the right instead?

Choose the right with all your might,
and things will go your way.
My CTR ring tells me so,
each and every day.

All at once, it's sitting there,
right before my eyes.
My best friend's birthday money,
in bills of ones and fives.

But my parents always taught me,
and I know that it is true,
it's wrong to take what isn't mine,
Oh, now, what shall I do?

Choose the wrong and not be fair—
Or choose the right and leave it there?

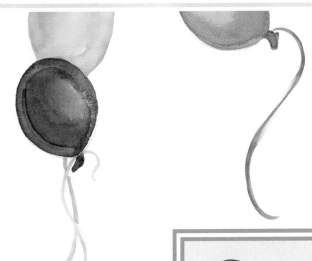

Choose the right with all your might,
and things will go your way.
My CTR ring tells me so,
each and every day.

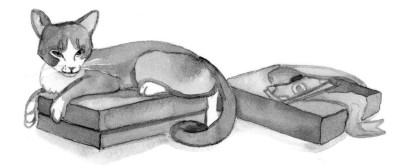

I heard the "big boys" talking
when I was in the yard.
I want to be a big boy, too,
I'm trying very hard.

The big boys sometimes say bad words
that Dad says I can't say . . .
But maybe if I talk like them,
they'll let me come and play.

Choose the wrong
and feel real bad—
Or choose the right,
and please my dad?

Choose the right with all your might,
and things will go your way.
My CTR ring tells me so,
each and every day.

I thought that we were joking,
but then Jack pushed me down.
I want to push him back so hard
it knocks him to the ground!

But if I do he'll get back up,
and we'll start throwing punches,
saying things like, "I hate you!"
and grabbing hair in bunches.

Choose the wrong and get all muddy—
Or choose the right and keep my buddy?

Choose the right with all your might,
and things will go your way.
My CTR ring tells me so,
each and every day.

Oh no!" My heart began to sink
when I looked at the test.
"I forgot to study
so I won't do my best."

But I can see Suzanne's desk,
she sits across the way.
And if I copy off her page,
I just might get an "A."

Choose the wrong and be afraid—
Or choose the right and earn my grade?

Choose the right with all your might,
and things will go your way.
My CTR ring tells me so,
each and every day.

When my mom left she gave a list
of chores for me to do.
The babysitter's on the phone
and doesn't have a clue.

So I could play, just play all day,
and ignore that silly list.
But when my mom gets home tonight,
she'll see the things I've missed.

Do I choose the wrong and just have fun—
Or choose the right and get things done?

Choose the right with all your might,
and things will go your way.
My CTR ring tells me so,
each and every day.

When I see my CTR ring
so shiny and so bright,
it helps me to remember
to always choose the right.

Your CTR ring helps you
remember what is right.
So when it's time to make a choice,
choose the right with all your might!